Wishing You a
'Merry Christmas'

F. Bright Owls Nursery

For Kevin, who loves Christmas!
with love, Giles

For Father Christmas,
with love, Emma

ORCHARD BOOKS
338 Euston Road, London NW1 3BH
Orchard Books Australia
Level 17/207 Kent Street, Sydney, NSW 2000

First published in 2013 by Orchard Books
First published in paperback in 2014

ISBN 978 1 40836 128 3

A CIP catalogue record for this book is available from the British Library.

1 3 5 7 9 10 8 6 4 2

Printed in China

Orchard Books is a division of Hachette Children's Books, an Hachette UK Company.
www.hachette.co.uk

I love you Father Christmas

Giles Andreae & Emma Dodd

ORCHARD

I love you, Father Christmas,

In your big red suit,

With your bright silver buckle

And your black shiny boots.

Your beard

looks amazing,

And, yes, you're

rather fat . . .

. . . But you probably just like eating,

And there's nothing wrong with that!

I love your pretty reindeer,

Flying fast across the skies . . .

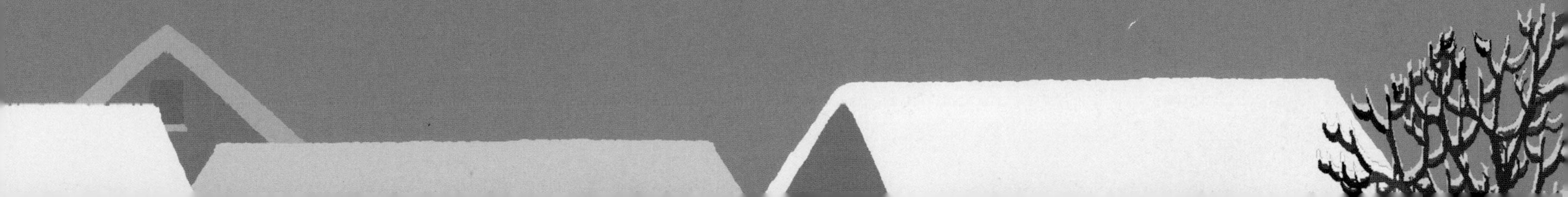

. . . I'll leave them all some carrots

And some yummy mince pies.

I love you, Father Christmas,

And I promise I've been good.

And I'm not just saying that

Because I know that I should.

I've tried every day

To be as helpful as can be.

I've said my 'please' and 'thank you's

And I always eat my tea.

I've played very nicely

With all the girls and boys.

I've kept my bedroom tidy

And I've tried to share my toys.

And I know I'm very lucky

With the way my life has been

But, it's just . . . I do like presents,

If you're getting what I mean?

So, lovely Father Christmas,
If you visit us tonight,
I swear there'll be no peeping
And we'll switch off every light.

Yes, I love you, Father Christmas,

You're the best, you are! Yippee!

Oh, I hope you like this letter . . .

With lots of love

from ME! xxx